Germs

By Martin Howard

Illustrated by Colin Stimpson

This paperback edition first published in the United Kingdom in 2011 by

Pavilion Children's Books
10 Southcombe Street
London
W14 0RA

An imprint of Anova Books Company Ltd

ISBN: 978-1-84365-185-7

A CIP catalogue record for this book is available from the British Library.

10 9 8 7 6 5 4 3 2 1

Reproduction by Dot Gradations Ltd, UK
Printed and bound by 1010 Printing International Ltd, China

This book can be ordered direct from the publisher at the website: www.anovabooks.com,
or try your local bookshop.

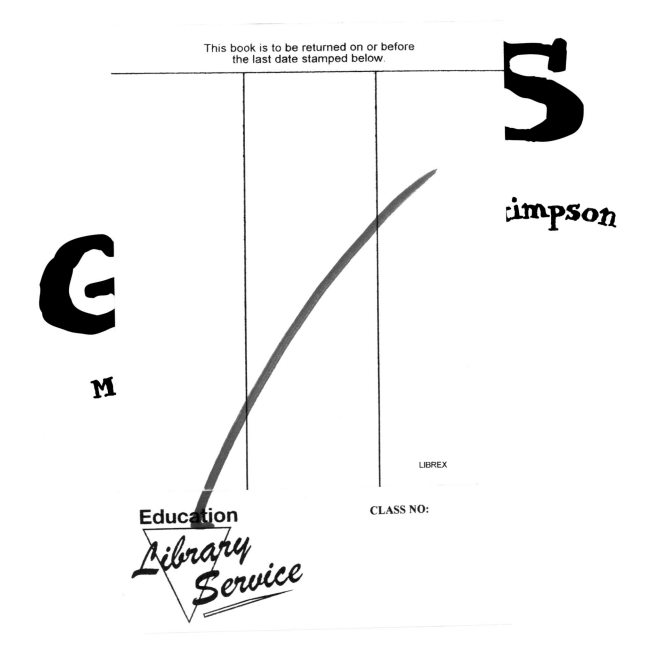

This book is to be returned on or before
the last date stamped below.

G

M

S

impson

LIBREX

CLASS NO:

Hold your nose and look down your toilet. If it's been cleaned, it may look shiny and it may not even smell too bad, but don't be fooled for a second. They're there. Germs. Millions and bezillions of them. Too small for you to see, but gazing up at you whenever you go to the toilet. They're too small to bite your bottom, but they would if they could because the germs don't like you. Not one little bit. They're not cute. They're definitely not fluffy. In fact, they'll make you feel quite ill.

All of them except one...

I'm just a tiny little germ and I didn't want to fight, so I hid around the U-bend, and shook with fright. That's where they found me — Queen Bacteria's police —

THE DREADED VIRALS.

"EVERY germ in the Toilet has to fight," the biggest one said.

"We have to make The Giant sick."

"But I like The Giant," I managed to say. "I like the sound of his funny voice, I like the fluffy paper that he throws at us and I don't want to do him any harm."

"You cowardly germ, what's your name?" the Viral asked.

"S...S...S...Sam," I said.

"Well, you're in the army now Sam!"

He grabbed me by the arm and dragged me off to Sergeant Botti, to become a fighting germ.

Sergeant Botti looked me up and down and said,

"Oh dear, oh dear, what have we here?"

"Umm, hello. I'm Sam," I replied.

"That's 'umm, hello Sarge,' you 'orrible germ!" he bellowed back.

"You're one of Botti's soldiers now. Are you ready to serve the Queen?"

"Errrr no, I'd rather not," I said.

"WHAT?!"

"Errrr no, I'd rather not, Sarge."

"Right. Now what kind of weapon shall we give you? A sword? No, too big for you... Bow and arrow? No, you're a germ for a spear if ever I saw one."

"Can't I stand at the back and cheer?" I asked. Botti laughed and jammed a helmet on my head.

"Oh no, you'll be right in the middle of the battle Private Sam...

...now off you go."

I didn't like training very much.

To prepare for battle I had to CHARGE and YELL at the top of my lungs...

...and do PRESS-UPS

...and SIT-UPS.

The weapons were BIG and HEAVY...

...and I would always end up in a TANGLE!

So, why are we going to war?" I asked.

"It's very simple," he said. "We try to make The Giant ill. King Antibod and his army will try to stop us but there will be too many of us, because The Giant doesn't..."

Suddenly, a shadow fell across the Toilet.

"**There he is! Up there! The Giant!**" Botti shouted.

"**Remember – It is every germ's duty to make him sick.**"

I peered upwards. "But why?" I asked again.

"**Because Queen Bacteria says so,**" Botti said. "**Now watch.**"

The sky went dark as The Giant's bum blocked out the light.
There was a splash, then The Giant stood and huge squares of soft, white paper floated down.

"**...And now the Flush!**" Botti roared. "**Everybody duck!**"

Water poured from above.
When it was over a voice
called from far, far away,

"BREEEEAKFAST IS REAAADY, BEN."

"COMING MUUUM."

The Giant boomed.
The Giant pulled his
pants up and
was gone.

"See what Sarge?" I asked.
Sergeant Botti looked down
at me and said,

"Did you see?" screamed Botti.

"Prepare for war, you grotty little germ...
The Giant didn't wash his hands."

Next day our orders came and off to war we went. Flags were waved and our swords and armour shone. And as we marched towards the Toilet Seat, Sergeant Botti made us sing.

"I don't know, but I've been told

♫

"...we make bottoms go all runny

"One, two, three, four.

♫

♫ ♫ ♫

♫

...he germs of Toy-o-let are bold..."

'Cos for germs it's really funny."

One, two, three, four. One, two, three, four."

♫

Finally, we made it to camp. Before me were millions and millions of germs and in the middle of the crowd, Queen Bacteria sat on her throne.

Every germ was silent as the Queen opened her mouth to speak.

"**Germs!** My devoted subjects, my crawling, slimy followers. We must make The Giant **ill!** Make his stomach **squelch** and green bubbles come out of his nose. Give him **headaches** and shivers and sore throats and every **disgusting** sickness we can think of!"

The whole army cheered. Except me.

"All that stands in our way is King Antibod and his army. **They must be destroyed!**"

All around me germs cheered again. Queen Bacteria looked down from her throne.

"To war then, my filthy germs!"

As the Toilet shook with cheers once more, the sky went dark. The Giant sat down with his hands resting on the Toilet Seat.

The great germ army marched to The Giant's hand and climbed on.

Behind me the Sergeant shouted, "onwards to glory Special Giant Attack Squad!"

and we sang...

"The germs of Toy-o-let love war. we're going to make this Giant sore. Antibod's troops are going to run, Just like this big old Giant's bum. one, two, three, four. one, two, three, four!"

Then we were carried high in the air on The Giant's hand and I could see all the Toilet below. For a moment the army held its breath. If The Giant washed his hands now it would mean the end of us. We'd all be swept into the Great Basin in a flood of soap and water. But instead, he just picked up the Toothbrush and a huge mouth opened before us. Suddenly, we were charging towards the enemy. The army of King Antibod.

"All you poopheads shake with **fear**, the germs of Toy-o-let are **here!**"

Sergeant Botti shouted, running past me with an axe in both hands.

"Charge, Private Sam! Charge!"

Then a Viral kicked me from behind, shouting

"Fight you coward. Fight for your Queen."

Suddenly all around was war. Whirling swords went zzZHHHHWUMMMMMMMMM! and arrows went

VIP! VIP! VIP!

I closed my eyes and lifted my spear. My knees were knocking and my teeth chattered with fear. I staggered forwards and a huge club bounced off my helmet. In the middle of the crashing smashing battle I fell and thought I must be dead.

I was still alive, though my head hurt and my spear was lost, so I began to crawl away through the legs of germs still fighting as fast as I could go. Very soon I had to stop. Something blocked the way. It was Sergeant Botti, laying there covered in bruises and cuts.

"Sarge!" I shouted. "Can you walk?"

Botti turned his head and looked at me with a tear in his eye. Then he croaked,

"Private Sam, I'm doomed. Doomed, I tell you...

...but there's still time for you."

He clutched at my hand and said,

"All my life I've been a soldier, and I never stopped to think. I could have had a wife and little germs, but I chose to attack a Giant who's never done us any ha.... Run away, Private Sam, r............o."

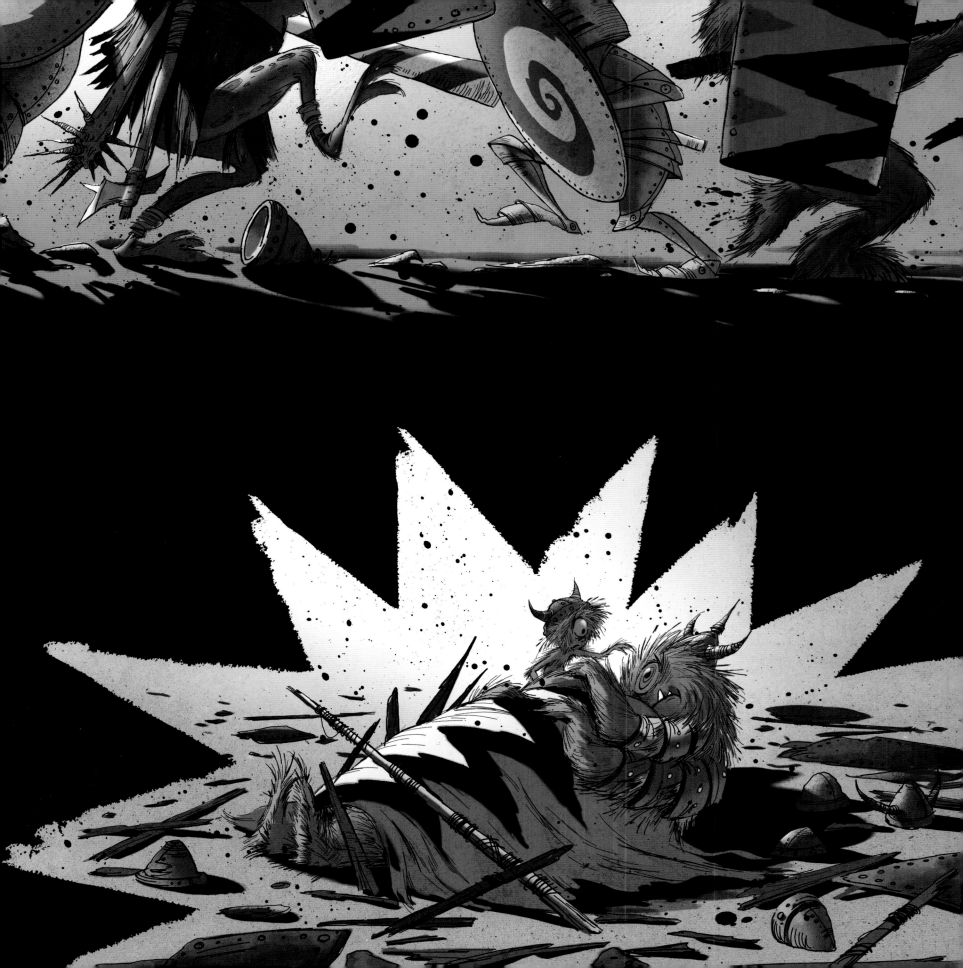

I ran, but the Virals caught me again and pushed me back into battle.
The fighting was fierce. There was screaming and shouting and farting.
Through the noise and the smell, Queen Bacteria screamed:

"Stomp them!"
"Chomp them!"
"Beat them up!"

I was lost. I couldn't fight. I was shivering and I'd dropped my spear again.

Then a hand pulled me away from the fighting and a voice spoke in my ear,
"You're my prisoner now, what's your name?" It was a girl soldier from the Antibod army.
"I...I'm Sam, please don't hurt me." I said. "I didn't want to come here. I'm a good germ really."
"If you're such a good germ why do you want to make The Giant sick?" she asked.
"I don't," I said. "But no one would listen."

"I'm Ella, of the King's Elite Giant Protection Squad," she said.
"And it sounds as if you're on the wrong side."

Well, she looked like a germ but she couldn't be.
She was kind and pretty and she smiled at me. I smiled back.
As I looked into her big blue eye I forgot all about the war.

I was in love.

...And then she blinked and I could hear fighting again.

Close by King Antibod shouted,

"Beat the germs back. Clean them out.!
Wash them away. Send them back to their Toilet."

It looked like the King's army was winning
but the Queen wasn't finished yet.

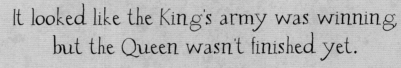

"Germs! Down the throat
and into the tummy!" she called.

"NO!"

cried Ella,

"We can't let them get to the
tummy! There will be sick
all over the place!"

Now I knew what I should do. I picked up a sword and whirled it around my head. All at once I wasn't afraid. "For King Antibod," I shouted. "For soap and water. For washing hands, and for a pine fresh Toilet." And with Ella by my side, I attacked.

As I might have mentioned once before, I'm just a tiny germ, but now I was with Ella I felt a thousand times as tall. Before me germs ran away. But I could still see Queen Bacteria, on a tooth high above, and I had an idea to put an end to her once and for all. So I charged at the Queen shouting a new battle cry: "Bacteria shake with fear, Private Sam's going to kick your REAR!"

"You traitor," Queen Bacteria shouted down as I got closer.

"I'll have you flushed for this! I'll watch you vanish around the bend."

"Oh shut up, you ugly old heap of plop!" I shouted back. "You're not wanted here."

"How dare you speak to your Queen like that?" she screeched.

"You're not my Queen you're a pest, a health hazard, a dirty speck of stinky grime," I replied and ran at her with arms outstretched. "And I've come to clean you up."

As she tried to get away, she screamed:

"what are you doing? No, you fool..."

I roared as I ran. "CHAAAAARGE!"

I felt her stumble

and pushed her hard...

...she s l i p p e d. She fell.

Queen Bacteria tumbled off the tooth and into the basin below

where a whirlpool carried her away, still screaming in the foamy water.

And as The Giant's mouth closed, I looked up and shouted as loud as I could.

"And by the way you silly Giant, you should

ALWAYS

WASH

YOUR

HANDS!"

With Queen Bacteria gone all of her germs ran away.

I was taken to King Antibod, who shook my hand until I thought it might come off. "Well done young germ! Well done indeed," he said. "You're a hero now you know. The Giant is safe once more. Name your reward young Sam, whatever we have is yours."

I looked into Ella's big blue eye. She looked back at me.
"Would it be alright if I stayed?" I asked. "I promise I won't make anyone sick."
"Of course, my boy," King Antibod said, "You'll always have a home here."
"Oh," I said. "And if by chance there's another war...

...can I just stand at the back and cheer?"

And that's how I
became an Antibodee far
away from where I was born.
Sometimes though, I look out of The
Giant's mouth at the land of Toilet
below watching the armies of
germs, training and waiting
for the day they can start
another war.

They'll keep
on trying all the time,
so if you're a Giant reading
this — be careful to wash your
hands. Just a splash of warm
water, some soap and a towel
will keep the germs away,
and you'll smell
nice too.

But now I've got to go. I'm getting married, you see...

everyone will cheer:

"Congratulations Sam n' Ella!"